# JR. CHAPTER BOOK

## THE BAILEY SCHOOL KIDS®

# GHOSTS DO SPLASH IN PUDDLES

# JR. CHAPTER BOOK
## THE BAILEY SCHOOL KIDS®

# GHOSTS DO SPLASH IN PUDDLES

by Marcia Thornton Jones and Debbie Dadey
Illustrated by Joëlle Dreidemy

SCHOLASTIC INC.
New York  Toronto  London  Auckland  Sydney
Mexico City  New Delhi  Hong Kong  Buenos Aires

To Anna Richardson, who knows how to keep
the ghosts from haunting our office! — M.J.

To Mrs. Sawin and the kids at Shepardson
Elementary in Fort Collins, Colorado. — D.D.

For Clement, my buddy and flatmate who looks like
Mister Shadow when he gets up in the morning! — J.D.

ISBN-10: 0-439-87629-X
ISBN-13: 978-0-439-87629-2

Text copyright © 2006
by Marcia Thornton Jones
and Debra S. Dadey
Illustrations copyright © 2006 by Scholastic Inc.
All rights reserved. Published by Scholastic Inc.

12 11 10 9 8                    9 10 11 12 13/0

Printed in the U.S.A.
First printing, September 2006

# CONTENTS

# 1

# EDDIE THE BRAVE

*Ooooooooo!*
*Oooooooooooooooo!*
*OOOOOOOOOOOOOO!*
   "Did you hear that?" Eddie
asked his three best friends.

Melody, Liza, Howie, and Eddie stood in the hall of Bailey School. They looked at the door to the boys' bathroom. The rest of the second graders were already in the lunchroom.

"It sounded like a g-gh-ghost!" Liza said. Her voice shook and her face was as pale as milk.

"Don't be silly," Eddie said. "There are no such things as ghosts. Even if there were, I'm sure there is no such thing as a bathroom ghost."

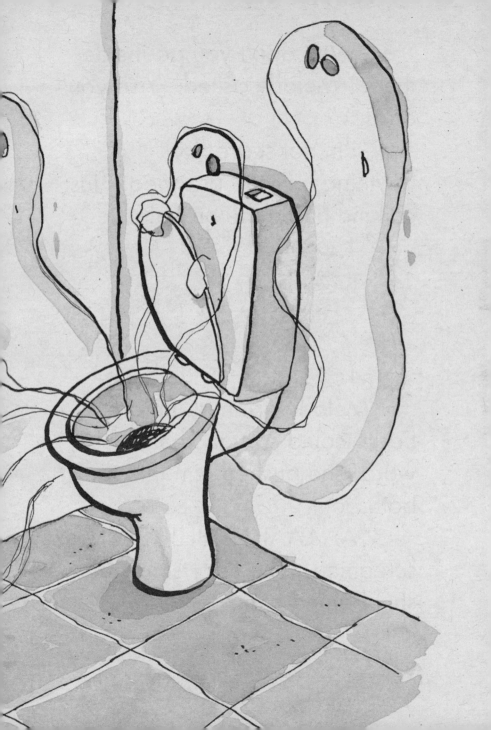

"Why don't you go inside then?" Melody asked. "Are you afraid?"

"I'm not scared of anything," Eddie bragged. "Just call me Eddie the Brave!"

Melody grinned. Before Eddie could say another word, she pushed him into the bathroom.

"AAAAAHHHHH!" Eddie screamed. The door slammed shut behind him.

# 2

# TRUE FRIENDS

Melody, Liza, and Howie put their ears against the door. "Maybe a monster ate him," Liza told Howie.

Melody shook her head. "No, a monster would spit him out. He'd taste bad."

YUK

"You shouldn't have pushed Eddie," Howie told Melody. Liza nodded. "Friends don't push."

"Eddie?" Howie whispered. "Are you okay?" He opened the door a crack.

Eddie didn't answer.
Instead, the lights flashed on
and off. All the toilets flushed at
once. Paper towels flew across
the floor and wrapped around
Howie's foot. A storm was
blowing in the boys' bathroom!

"Watch out!" Melody yelled
as Eddie ran out the door. Eddie
and Howie fell. They tumbled
across the floor.

They rolled right into
Principal Davis.
Eddie gulped.
Howie moaned.
Melody gasped.
Liza cried.

gulp!

moan!

gasp!

waaa!

What would Principal Davis do? He looked in the bathroom. Puddles were under the sinks. Puddles were on the floor. Puddles were everywhere!

# 3

## SQUEAK!

"Did you hear that?"
Liza gulped.
*Squeakkkk!*
*Squeeeeeaaaaak!*
*SQUEEEAAAAAKKKK!*
It sounded like rusty chains
rattling in a haunted house.

"You'd have to be on Mars not to hear that noise. I wonder what it is," Melody said.

The two girls were sitting at the lunch table with Howie and Eddie.

Eddie grinned. Peanut
butter covered his front teeth.
Peanut butter dotted his nose.
Peanut butter was stuck to his
baseball cap. "It sounds like the
bathroom ghost is rattling his

chains in the hall."

Liza stuck her tongue out at Eddie. She didn't like anything scary, especially ghosts. "Friends shouldn't scare each other," she told him.

"Don't worry," Howie said after taking a sip of milk. "Ghosts are only in stories. They aren't real."

"Then who made all those puddles?" Eddie asked. "It wasn't me, even if Principal Davis won't believe me."

"There must be a leak in the water pipes," Melody said.

Liza nodded, but Eddie wasn't giving up. "I think you're wrong," he said. "Bailey School has a puddle ghost and he's right here."

He has my HAT!

He has my ARM!

He has my NECK!

I can't stop HIM!

Eddie's hand came down and landed hard on a ketchup bottle. It squirted all over Liza.

# 4

# SHADOW

A big white hand gripped Eddie's shoulders. He stopped eating and looked up into the palest face he'd ever seen. Dark shadows made his eyes look like holes. His eyes were so light they looked yellow.

Liza looked at the face and screamed. "It's the ghost!"

Eddie gulped. His shoulder felt ice-cold. "Who are you?"

"My name is Mr. Shadow,"

said the strange man. When he
smiled, his big eyes seemed to
glow. "I do not like this mess."
    "It was worse when he shot
peas with his straw," Liza said.

Mr. Shadow's hands went to his cheeks. "*Noooo,*" he gasped.

"This wasn't as bad as the time he squirted syrup on the ceiling," Howie said.

Mr. Shadow held both sides of his head "*Nooooooooo,*" he groaned.

"I think the worst thing he did was put mustard on the teacher's chair," Melody added.

Mr. Shadow
moaned even louder.
"NOOOOOOOOOOOO!"

Mr. Shadow walked away. He shook his head and kept moaning.

"He must be a new lunchroom helper," Melody said. "He acts weird."

"He's strange," Howie said.

Eddie saw his chance to tease Liza. He lowered his voice and wiggled his fingers in front of Liza's eyes.

"That's no lunchroom helper. That's THE PUDDLE GHOST!"

# 5

# SCHOOL-EATING GHOSTS

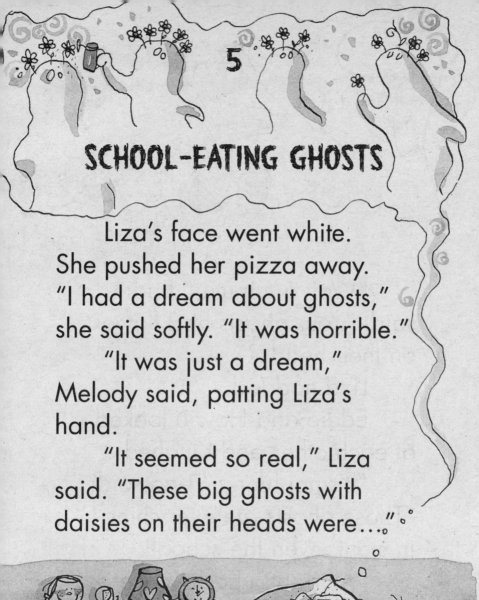

Liza's face went white. She pushed her pizza away. "I had a dream about ghosts," she said softly. "It was horrible."

"It was just a dream," Melody said, patting Liza's hand.

"It seemed so real," Liza said. "These big ghosts with daisies on their heads were...."

"Wait a minute," Eddie said. "Your ghosts had flowers on their heads?"

Liza nodded.

Eddie and Howie looked at each other and laughed.

"It's not funny," Liza said. "Those ghosts ate everything in sight, even the school!"

"All right!" Eddie cheered. "I like these ghosts."

CRUNCH

"But what if the puddle ghost is like the ghosts in my dream?" Liza said.

"A school-eating ghost would be great!" Eddie said.

Liza shook her head. "These ghosts also ate TV's and all the candy."

Eddie's eyes opened wide and he yelled, "We have to stop the puddle ghost!"

# 6

# BELLY GHOST

Mr. Shadow came up behind Eddie and glared at the kids. "Shhh," he warned them and then drifted away to another table. "*Noooooooo* yelling."

"Could he really be a ghost?" Liza asked.

"There must be a way to tell," Eddie said.

Howie nodded. "I know a way. In the stories I've read, ghosts are never solid. You can see through them, and you can throw things through them. You can even put your hand through them."

"You mean if our hands go right through his belly, we'll know he's a ghost?" Melody said.

Liza's face was as white as her milk. "Yuck!" Liza said. "I'm NOT doing it."

Eddie grinned. "I will. But you have to come with me."

"No, we don't," Liza told Eddie.

"Yes, you do," Eddie said. "You always say friends stick together. Now you have to decide. Are you REALLY my friend?"

Friends
stick TOGETHER !

EXTRA STRONG GLUE.

FOR FRIENDS ONLY

Howie stood up. "Of course we're your friends."

Melody stood up. "We're best friends."

The three friends looked at Liza. Liza sighed. Then she stood up. "Let's get this ghost test over with once and for all!"

# 7
# THE TEST

Eddie ran around a table. He zipped past a chair. His three friends were right behind him. Eddie's hand was almost to Mr. Shadow's back.

Just then, Mr. Shadow turned around. His hollow eyes glared at Eddie. A chair slid across the floor without any help. Eddie's shoelace got tangled on the chair.

BAM! Eddie stumbled over the chair.

SPLAT! Melody tripped over Eddie.

CRASH! Howie slid into a stack of trays.

PLOP! Liza fell on top.

They all landed in a
big pile.

"Uh-oh," Eddie said as he
pulled a noodle out of his hair.
Liza, Melody, Eddie, and
Howie looked up. Mr. Shadow
towered over them. That's not all
they saw.

Principal Davis stood next to
Mr. Shadow.

# 8

# GHOST STORM

Eddie sat in Principal Davis's office. Liza, Melody, and Howie sat with him. They waited for Principal Davis.

"I hope you're happy," Liza said with a sniff. "I've heard that kids fall into a deep pit in here. No one ever sees them again."

"It wasn't my fault," Eddie snapped. "That chair moved all by itself."

"How can a chair move on its own?" Melody asked.

"It can't," Howie said slowly. "It had help. Ghost help."

"What are you talking about?" Melody asked.

Howie looked at the closed door to make sure no one else could hear.

"I think Mr. Shadow *is* a ghost and he made that chair move so Eddie couldn't prove it."

"You said there are no such things as ghosts," Liza told Howie.

"Maybe I was wrong," Howie said.

"Don't be silly," Melody said. "Ghosts don't work in school lunchrooms."

"This ghost does," Eddie said. And he also jumps in puddles. He's the one that

No way it's a real ghost.

Sure is!

caused trouble for me in the bathroom and now he's causing trouble in the lunchroom. But that's the last time he gets me in trouble. I'm going to stop this ghost once and for all!"

Just then the windows flew open. Desk drawers slid open all on their own. Papers zipped through the air.

"It's a ghost storm!" Liza screamed as Principal Davis walked into his office.

# 9

# BAD IDEA

The next day, Eddie tapped the lunchroom table with his fingers. He banged his fork on the bench.

He was so mad he couldn't sit still. He felt like steam was coming out of his ears. He had to get the puddle ghost.

"Principal Davis thinks we made that mess yesterday," Liza said. "Now, it's no recess for a week!"

| | |
|---|---|
| MONDAY | RECESS |
| TUESDAY | RECESS |
| WEDNES. | RECESS |
| THURSDAY | RECESS |
| FRIDAY | RECESS |
| SAT. | |
| SUN. | |

"The puddle ghost made that mess!" Howie said.

Melody shook her head. "It was only the wind."

"It was the ghost," Eddie said. For Eddie, no recess was worse than having all his teeth pulled. He wanted to get even.

Liza took a big bite of green Jell-O and a sip of milk. It gave Eddie an idea. A bad idea. The worst idea ever.

# 10

# SLIME

"If the puddle ghost wants puddles," Eddie said, "maybe we should give him puddles."

I will give him PUDDLES!

"Eddie," Howie said. "What are you talking about?"

Eddie grinned an evil smile.

That made Liza worried.
Very worried.

"Uh-oh," she said. "That's
how Eddie looked right before
he tripped the school bully."

"He looked the same way when he let all the hamsters out of their cages," Howie added.

"He smiled that way just before he put itching powder in the art box," Melody added.

"Don't do it," Liza told him. "We're in enough trouble already."

Eddie picked up his chocolate milk. He planned to splash milk all over Mr. Shadow's feet. It was a bad plan. A very bad plan, but Eddie ended up doing something even worse. Eddie looked at Mr. Shadow. He was carrying a pile of dirty plates toward the kitchen. Eddie walked toward Mr. Shadow.

"Stop!" Melody said, grabbing Eddie's arm.

STOP!

55

"Leave me alone," Eddie said. He pulled away from Melody. He didn't see the lunchroom lady in front of him.

Eddie's arm jerked into the lady. He knocked into the big pan of Jell-O she was carrying.

"Sorry," Eddie said, but it was too late. The pan of Jell-O flew into the air.

It flew over
Melody's head. It
soared like a green

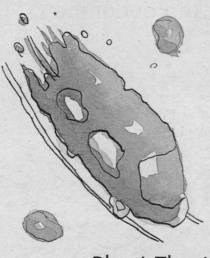

jet plane.
"Yikes!"
Howie yelled.
The green Jell-O
shot toward
Mr. Shadow
like a slime
train.

Plop! The Jell-O landed
on Mr. Shadow's brown shoes.
Mr. Shadow picked up his foot.
He stomped in the Jell-O. He
splashed in the Jell-O.

It splashed on Eddie.

It splashed on Melody.
It splashed on Howie.
It splashed on Liza.
"That's it! I quit!" cried Mr.
Shadow as he slinked out of the
lunchroom.

# NO RECESS

At recess, Eddie didn't play kickball.

At recess, Melody didn't run races.

At recess, Liza didn't swing on the swings.

At recess, Howie didn't read a book.

Instead, they wiped Jell-O off the floor. They wiped Jell-O off the wall. They even wiped Jell-O off the lunch lady.

"This is the worst recess ever," Eddie said.

"At least Mr. Shadow disappeared after the Jell-O

mess," Melody said. "He just couldn't put up with Eddie's messes."

"Or," Liza said softly, "maybe he was a ghost after all and Eddie discovered the one thing ghosts can't stand. Jell-O slime."

"If Liza's right," Howie said, "then ghosts really do splash in puddles."

Eddie sat up straight. He puffed out his chest. "I saved Bailey School from the puddle ghost. Now Liza has nothing to fear."

Liza looked at Eddie.

"You did that for me? You really are a good friend," she told Eddie. "Thank you."

And then Liza gave Eddie a great big hug.